D1241091

TAILS OF
JAXX
IN
BARKHAMSTED

The town's pets are vanishing.
Will he solve the mystery in time?

Joanna Lee Doster

TAILS OF JAXX IN BARKHAMSTED
Copyright © 2019 by Joanna Lee Doster

MPI
PUBLISHING

Publisher: MPI Publishing
ISBN-13: 978-0-9960179-6-1 (hc)
ISBN-10: 0-9960179-6-8 (hc)
Library of Congress Control Number: 2019902170
Cover and interior design: One of a Kind Covers
Visit the author at:
https://authorjdoster.wixsite.com/joannaleedoster

First Edition

TAILS OF
JAXX
IN
BARKHAMSTED

Joanna Lee Doster

MPI
PUBLISHING

Dedication

This book is dedicated to the memory of
Beau, our beloved Maltese dog and loyal
companion for almost eleven years. His soul
was larger than life only matched by his
endless capacity to love. We take solace in
knowing that he's now reunited with his
brother, Jumping Jack Flash, in Heaven.

Also by Joanna Lee Doster

Tails Of Jaxx At The Metropolitan Opera

Contents

Chapter One

I had to keep my promise to Rufus. A promise is a promise. It was up to me to help find Aunt Lulu's cat. And when the next day turned into night, and Mikey was still missing, I made my move. I waited until everyone was asleep at Aunt Lulu's and snuck out through the kitchen doggie door. Earlier, my bulldog friend Rufus, had showed me the spot where I could wiggle under the backyard fence.

I don't like it when I don't know where I am going.

It was bone chilling November cold. The blast of frigid air hit my face like a snowball. The moon was covered by a gauzy veil of clouds. Patches of starlight led my way around drifts of snow. Shadows of trees snaked across white blanketed lawns. Only quiet and darkness kept me company. I wished Rufus was with me. I was so scared, but I still had to find Mikey. I remembered how terrible it was when I got lost during a blizzard and was separated from my parents for a long time. I walked around the trees and hedges leading into the neighbor's pitch black yard. Then, I trotted up a hill to the next street.

"OWW! OWWW!" I let out a whimper.

The crunchy snow and ice burned my paws and made them sting. It was silent except for the loud thumping of my heart.

I missed the constant noise of New York City, where I live with my parents. It's the best city in the world, especially for a dog like me. The blaring traffic sounds of cars, buses and trucks had always kept me company. I was used to seeing the bright lights of the city, even at night.

I waited and listened for any sounds of Mikey. A dark animal with a white stripe on his back slipped by me. "EWWW!" I recognized his foul smell. It was a skunk. I had seen one in Central Park once. I dodged out of his way, so I wouldn't become the target of his stinky spray. There was a bark of a lonely dog far away. But then, I heard it.

"Meow. Meow."

I froze in my tracks.

Could it be Mikey?

I followed the scent a few more blocks to the front steps of a house. After sniffing around, the trail went cold. *Where could he have gone?*

I had to get back to Aunt Lulu's before someone discovered I was missing. And, before my toes got frostbitten.

Maybe Mikey doubled back and went home and I won't have to sneak out again!

My name is Jumping Jaxx. I am a seven-year-old Maltese dog.

How did I ever get here?

Chapter Two

It all began a few days before. Dad, Mom and I were waiting in line for a train in New York City's Grand Central Station. We were going on holiday to visit Dad's sister, Aunt Lulu, who lived in Barkhamsted, Connecticut.

Grand Central Station is the largest train terminal in the world. It's always teeming with people traveling to places all over. When our train pulled into the platform, the doors opened and we boarded. Mom took an aisle seat. Dad took one by the window. I was in my crate on Mom's lap. There were lots of people; some sitting alone, some with families and some with small animals in crates, too.

"Hello folks," said the conductor. He was dressed in a blue uniform with a matching cap. "Got your tickets?" Dad handed him ours. The conductor punched holes in them and handed them back to Dad. He moved on to the next row.

As we rode into the countryside, our train sped by snow covered houses and trees and cars driving along roads.

I wonder who lives in those places. Do they have a dog like me?

Chug- Chug- Chug-a-Chug. The train was rocking steadily along. It stopped every once in a while to let passengers get on and off. At one stop, a boy got on and sat down in an aisle seat across from us. He waved to someone out the window. When he took off his bulky purple backpack, it thumped down into the seat. It looked like he had stuffed everything he had into it. He reached into the backpack and pulled out a game. I watched him play until I nodded off.

When I woke up, Mom took me out of my crate and cuddled me in her arms.

The boy looked at me and smiled. Then, he got up and walked over to us.

"May I pet your dog?" he asked Mom.

"Sure."

"What's his name?"

"Jaxx."

"Isn't he a Maltese?"

"Why yes, he is. How did you know?"

"I read in a book they're one of the oldest breeds. I love all kinds of animals."

He patted my head.

"Hiya Jaxx."

"What's your name?" said Mom.

"Oh, I'm Colin."

"Nice to meet you, Colin. I'm Kathryn and this is my husband, Thomas."

Just then, the conductor's loud voice boomed, "Next stop, Shelton. There will be a twenty minute break so we can change locomotives. You can stretch your legs. When you hear the whistle blow get back on, or the train will leave without you!"

The train pulled to a stop. Colin gathered his things and got off. After we left the train, Mom and Dad sat on a bench along the platform. Dad set my crate down and started a conversation with one of the passengers.

The smell of chicken wafted toward my nose. I unclasped the hook on my crate door. It's a trick I learned a long time ago. It made Mom and Dad laugh. But this time, I didn't do it to be funny. I really wanted that chicken! It smells so good. *Hmmm. I know I shouldn't do it! But...* I wandered off dragging my leash away from the station. I found the chicken lying on the ground. I almost had it in my mouth when...

"Jaxx! No! Stop!" Colin yelled. "Don't eat that!" He grabbed my leash. "Let's go back."

"EHH! EHH! EHH!"

What was that?

Colin reached into his backpack and pulled out a pair of binoculars. He scanned the area.

"Come with me Jaxx!"

Still holding my leash, Colin darted down the stairs and out of the station to a park across the street. That's when I saw it. A fawn was stuck in a chain link fence. His hind quarters were wedged into a hole backwards.

"Ehh! Ehh!" cried the fawn.

One of his back legs was bruised. Colin tried to wrap his arms around the animal and gently pull him out. The fawn kicked and screamed louder.

"You'll be all right," he whispered to the shaking fawn. "I'm going to help you."

It cried and cried. Colin attempted to widen the hole in the metal fence with his pocket knife. I wanted to help, but I didn't know how. The hole wouldn't budge and the fawn was still struggling. I nosed through Colin's backpack and found a small metal container. It smelled like the hair gel Dad uses. I grasped the container in my mouth and dropped it at Colin's feet.

He picked it up and said, "Hmmm, this might work! Thanks, Jaxx."

He rubbed some on his hands. He massaged it all over where the fawn was stuck. Colin gently nudged the fawn backwards through the hole. The fawn did a backwards flip and landed upright on all four legs. Startled but free, it ran to its mother who had been hiding in the bushes nearby, anxiously watching and waiting. Together they sprinted off to the woods.

WOO-A-WOO-WOO!

CHUG – CHUG – CHUG

"OH NO!" Colin shouted. "The train! We gotta go back!"

Colin grabbed his backpack and scooped me up. He ran as fast as he could across the street and up the steps into the station. Dad and Mom looked frantic. They were standing beside my empty crate.

"JAXX! COLIN! Where were you?" Dad shouted. "You scared us! We've been searching all over!"

Colin was out of breath. He put me into Mom's arms, who squeezed me so tight my ribs hurt.

"I'm sorry," Colin explained, "but I caught Jaxx about to eat old chicken parts that were on the ground and I stopped him. And then, just as I was about to bring him back to you, I spotted a baby deer in danger and Jaxx helped me save it."

Colin told Mom and Dad what happened, while we waited for the next train. By the time it came, Dad had calmed down a little, but I could tell he was still upset with me about the chicken.

Chapter Three

W hen we arrived in Barkhamsted, Dad carried me, and the porter carried the rest of our things off the train. Colin got off after us.

Was Colin staying in Barkhamsted, too?

"Oh, yoo-hoo! Kathryn! Thomas! Over here."

It was Aunt Lulu, standing by a big red car, waving her hands. I recognized her from when she visited us in the city.

"I've missed you!" She hugged and kissed Mom and Dad and bent down to my crate and said, "Hello Jaxx, you cute thing."

Next to Aunt Lulu was a woman with white and black speckled hair.

"Thomas, Kathryn," Aunt Lulu said, this is my friend, Consuela Tarquin. She's waiting for her grandson."

Colin made a beeline for her.

"Grammy!"

She gave him a big hug.

"I missed you so much, Colin. Wait until the dogs see you!"

"Nice to meet you, Consuela," Dad said. "We met Colin on the train. Your grandson and our dog had quite an adventure."

"Look, Grammy! This is Jaxx, their Maltese."

Consuela knelt down and smiled at me. When she stood up she turned to Dad and said, "I'd love to hear all about their adventure. Won't you all come to my house for hot chocolate on your way to Lulu's?"

Aunt Lulu said, "Thank you, Consuela. We'd love to."

We piled into Aunt Lulu's car and trailed behind Colin's grandmother's SUV. Aunt Lulu talked a lot as she drove down tree lined streets, narrow roads and up the hills. It didn't look at all like New York City. There were only a few other cars on the road. A school bus and a mail truck passed by us. There were a lot of houses with pretty snow-covered yards and lots more trees. It looked like how Central Park would look if it had houses. But where were the tall buildings shooting up into the sky, the taxis, buses, noisy traffic and crowds of people?

Consuela drove around a large circular driveway and parked in front of a big house and got out. Aunt Lulu did the same.

Two big men, dressed in heavy coats, worked on clearing the snow and ice from around the house. Consuela and Colin were met by a man at the front door. Consuela turned around and waved us over. Everyone was introduced.

Philipe, Consuela's assistant said, "Please come in and warm up. Colin, why don't you take Jaxx out of his crate and get him some water."

Several barking Afghan dogs came bounding out to the front hall and jumped on everyone. Their long legs made them look gigantic. They had ivory colored hair that swayed back and forth when they moved. Colin rolled on the floor and played with them. They couldn't stop wagging their ring curl tails and offering loving licks.

"ZuZu! Bella! Angel! Teddy! I've missed you guys."

Colin hugged and petted them some more. Then, he took off.

Philipe took everyone's coats before walking the dogs back to their kennels.

"Philipe," Consuela said, "would you please bring some hot chocolate for my guests?" Then, she turned to us and said, "Come see my champion show dog, Annabella."

We followed her to a room where an Afghan dog was fast asleep in a blue velvet bed. Wow! I have the same bed at home.

"Annabella is going to have her pups soon. That's why I'm keeping her separated from the others," Consuela said.

I had never seen such a beautiful dog. She woke up and her pretty dark brown almond shaped eyes glistened, adding a glow to her sweet face. Her hair had a silky shine. When everyone left, I stayed behind.

"Oh-h, Oh-h," Annabella whimpered.

"Are you okay?"

Startled, she said, "Who are you?"

"I'm Jaxx. I'm here visiting."

"Oh-h, I don't feel well, Jaxx. My stomach hurts."

"Don't worry Annabella. You'll be fine."

"I hope so. I'm so tired."

"Can I come back and see you again?"

"That would be nice, Jaxx."

Annabella fell back to sleep.

I didn't want to leave her, but I knew she needed to rest.

The house was very big, almost like Grand Central. It had a winding staircase. There were large paintings of people and dogs. I found Colin and followed him into the kitchen. I lapped up most of the water in a bowl he had filled. Philipe prepared the hot chocolate. He leaned down and scratched me behind my ears. I smelled a lot of different dogs on him.

"Come with me, Jaxx." said Colin, as he scurried down a long hallway. He stopped in front of a room and turned on the light.

"This is my room."

I sniffed around. There was a large TV, and stacks of books. His backpack was on top of a dresser with clothes and things spilling out. There were pictures of animals on the walls. He turned on a computer and began talking to some people. You could see their faces.

"Mom, Dad, I'm in Grammy's house."

The people on the computer spoke to him.

He said, "Yes, Grammy's fine. The dogs are great. I met another dog, Jaxx, on the train."

He told them about the deer rescue. Then he paused and said, "I smell hot chocolate. I have to go! Love you." He turned off the computer. "Come on, Jaxx!"

We passed by an elevator, just like the ones in our apartment building.

An elevator in a house? Who else lives here?

Back in the living room, Consuela was showing pictures of her champion dogs.

"And here's a picture of Colin at the Westminster Dog Show with me and Annabella last year. In this one, Colin is training my dogs. I'm so happy he's spending the holidays with me. Did you know that Colin wants to be a veterinarian when he grows up?"

Philipe set down a tray with cups and a large pot on a table. He poured everyone a cup of hot chocolate. He handed me a doggie biscuit to nibble on. I was hungry. While they were talking and sipping their drinks, I napped on the rug by the warm fireplace. Colin sat next to me and petted me the whole time.

When it was time to go, Philipe brought out the coats.

Aunt Lulu said, "Thank you so much, Consuela. I am so glad I finally met you, Colin. Your grandmother talks about you all of the time."

Colin smiled and then put me back into my crate. "Bye, Jaxx."

I liked Colin. I hoped I'd get to see him again.

Chapter Four

A unt Lulu drove us up a long driveway. Her house was dark brown with lots of windows and had a wreath on the front door and holiday lights around the eaves. The trees and bushes all around her house were puffed up with pillows of snow. Nothing matched the way things were at home in the city. There were no sidewalks to walk on. All the houses on Aunt Lulu's street were close to a busy road. She pulled her car into a big garage that was attached to the house.

"This way," she said, as she helped carry the luggage through the connected basement and up the stairs to her house.

It wasn't like our apartment building, or Colin's grandmother's house. There was no elevator!

The smell of cookies and pie hit my nose as soon as we got inside her white and shiny kitchen.

"Look, Jaxx!" Aunt Lulu said. She pointed to a small cut out panel in her back door. "You can run in and out of this door when you want to go out and play in the backyard."

"MMMEORW!"

Aunt Lulu picked up a big black cat and stroked him.

"This is Mikey," she said.

Mikey just stared at me. When Aunt Lulu put him down, I inched forward and sniffed him.

Hmmm, He sort of smelled like my cat friend, Caramelo, back home.

Mikey hissed, then ran for the swinging panel in the back door. I followed him outside. A wooden fence surrounded a big yard. Mikey didn't stick around to play with me. Instead, he snuck away. *That's not very nice!*

The sun was setting. It got colder and darker. The sky and clouds seemed larger here than in the city. The silence was broken by strange sounds.

"Hoo! Hoo!"

It was an owl, who screeched a lot. A squirrel raced up a tree with an acorn in its mouth. A horse was neighing in the woods. I shivered. But not from the cold. *Everything is so different here.* Maybe different is okay. I'll just have to get used to new things.

"ARF, ARF! G-r-r-r... WOOF!" A great big dog had run up to the fence. His loud barking scared me.

"Who are you?" he growled.

"I'm Jaxx. Who are you?"

"I'm Rufus, I'm a bulldog," he said proudly in his gruff voice.

"Rufus, is that a horse I heard just now?"

"Yes, it's Tom Tom, Lulu's horse. She keeps him in a barn in the woods."

I liked horses. I knew a lot about them from my horse friends, Zeus and Apollo, at The Metropolitan Opera, where I lived for a while when I was lost.

"Jaxx!" Dad's voice startled me. "Time to come in," he shouted. "It's freezing out. Let's go!"

"Gotta go! Goodnight, Rufus."

"See you around," Rufus answered.

A gust of wind roared by. I turned to see the long branches of the tall trees swaying back and forth. I was glad the lights were on in Aunt Lulu's house. So many other houses were dark. It wasn't lit up like the city, at all. It was so different.

Mikey didn't come back. After I ate, I was snuggled up in a warm blanket on Aunt Lulu's sofa. The fire in her fireplace was crackling. Everything was so warm and cozy. It was a big room with a large screen television, like we had at home. But I was too tired to enjoy it.

"Looks like my pup is ready for bed," Dad said.

He carried me to a back bedroom. The fireplace in the bedroom was lit, too. Mom was already asleep. Dad surprised me and had brought my blue velvet doggie bed. I curled myself up in it and the last thing I thought about before I drifted off to sleep, was Annabella, the beautiful show dog.

Chapter Five

W hen I woke up the next morning, I heard Aunt Lulu crying. "Mikey is missing! He didn't come home this morning. Mikey loves to wander through the neighborhood all night. But he always comes back when I call him. This is the first time he didn't show up!"

Dad must have remembered how scared he was when I went missing.

"Get your coat, Lulu," he said. "Let's drive around and see if we can spot him."

He shook his finger at me and said, "Jaxx, you stay here. Don't you dare leave! I'll feed you when I get back."

I wanted to visit with Rufus but I knew Dad meant business. I waited until Dad left and then I let out a howl and a bark.

"O-oooow! Arf! Arf!"

"UGH! OOH! EEH!" wheezed Rufus. Was I surprised when I saw him wedge his bulldog body right through Aunt Lulu's little doggie door. He got stuck for a moment so he held his breath and squeezed as hard as he could.

"Hey Jaxx," said Rufus panting. "I've been waiting for you outside."

"My dad told me to stay in. Mikey didn't come home this morning. He's missing. They're out searching for him now."

"Oh, no! That's why I haven't seen him today. Mikey and I are best friends. Lulu got him the same time my family got me. We look out for each other, in our own way. He wanders around, but he always comes back home. If he doesn't show up soon, I'll have to track him down. Will you help me?"

"I promise I will, Rufus. But first, you'll have to show me around the neighborhood!"

Aunt Lulu's car pulled up in the driveway.

"Oh good! They're back. Rufus, you better go. I'll let you know if they found Mikey."

"Okay. And remember your promise, Jaxx. Bark, if you need me!"

Rufus squeezed his big body back out through the doggie door just as Mom, Dad and Aunt Lulu came into the kitchen. Mikey wasn't with them.

Dad hugged me. "Jaxx," he whispered in my ear, "I'm so glad you're safe!"

Chapter Six

T he next morning, the smells coming from the
kitchen and my empty stomach got me out of
bed. Aunt Lulu was still crying. Even with
everyone searching the day before, no one had any
luck finding Mikey.

"Lulu," said Dad, "let's make missing cat posters
for Mikey. I'll print out copies and we can put them

up around town. I'll need a picture of him. Do you have one?"

Lulu handed Mikey's picture to Dad.

Mom turned to Dad, "Lulu and I are going to check with the neighbors. Maybe they've seen Mikey."

While they were gone, Dad fed me and made the posters. He put me in my favorite red sweater and grabbed my leash. We went out and walked around town, putting posters up on lampposts, in stores, and at the fire station. Along the way, Dad searched behind bushes and trees.

"Mikey? Here, Mikey! Mikey, where are you?"

Dad stopped at an animal hospital. He put up Mikey's poster on the bulletin board.

"Wow, Jaxx. There sure are a lot of missing dog posters here!"

We walked back home. As we passed a house, I picked up a strong whiff of Mikey's scent. I yanked on the leash to follow it. Dad yanked the leash back and walked towards Lulu's house.

"Arf! Arf!"

"No, Jaxx. We're not going that way."

I kept tugging as hard as I could toward the scent, but he kept pulling me away.

"Come on, Jaxx! Let's go!" he shouted.

I had to figure out a way to check this out later.

When we reached Aunt Lulu's, Dad patted my head and said, "I couldn't bear it if you ever went missing again, Jaxx!"

Chapter Seven

"**M**om and Aunt Lulu aren't back yet," said Dad. "Let's go see Lulu's horse." The barn was in the woods, far back on Lulu's property. By the time we got there, I heard Tom Tom whinny. I was cold, but the barn was warm. Dad gave Tom Tom a piece of an apple.

"Here's a goody for you, old boy!" he said to Tom Tom.

Dad put me on a bench and took off my leash. He unlatched the stall and brought Tom Tom out into a big room. He found Tom Tom's grooming set and began brushing him. Tom Tom asked who I was. I told him some things about me and my life in New York City. And about my horse friends, Zeus and Apollo. Then I yawned, and started to doze off. I must have fallen asleep.

I woke up when Dad said, "We should go back, Jaxx."

Dad led Tom Tom to his stall and patted him good-bye.

"We'll come and see you again."

As we left the barn, an angry growl pierced the air. It was coming from the nearby woods.

"G-r-r-r! G-r-rowl!"

Dad froze. "Jaxx! Stay!"

Tom Tom neighed loudly. "It's that coyote again, Jaxx. She's looking for food. Be careful!"

Before Dad could put my leash back on, I took off in a flash and ran towards the coyote. I ran in circles around her and nipped at her hind legs. The coyote snarled and bared her teeth.

"Jaxx!" Dad screamed. "Stop!"

My heart was racing. The coyote sprang up and lunged at me. I darted out of the way. She tried to poke and claw at my face with her powerful paws.

"Gr-r-w!"

With a lot of force and fury the coyote aimed for my neck and side. Again and again, she rushed at me. I kept darting away to avoid her attacks. My sweater helped protect me.

"Arf! Arf! Arf! Arf! Arf!" I barked and barked until my throat hurt.

Her claws barely missed my shoulder. She kept pouncing and I kept dodging. I was getting tired. I took a deep breath. *I cannot give up.* When the coyote lunged at me again, I growled and snarled back. I retreated and placed myself between my dad and the coyote.

Tom Tom bolted out of the barn and was now charging toward the coyote.

"Ne-e-eigh! Ne-eigh! Get back, Jaxx!"

Tom Tom stomped his front hooves. He whinnied and reared up high over the coyote. He turned around to kick her with his hind legs. He must have clipped her, because she ran off into the woods, yipping and whining.

Dad grabbed me and checked me over from head to tail. He wouldn't stop hugging me.

"Jaxx, don't you ever do that again! I don't know if my heart will ever stop beating so fast."

Dad hugged Tom Tom's neck.

"I'm going to make sure my sister gives you a wonderful dinner," he said, as he walked Tom Tom back to his stall.

Tom Tom winked at me. "Try to stay out of trouble, Jaxx!"

I was still shaking. "I will. And thank you for saving my life!"

Chapter Eight

I t was getting dark out and Mikey still hadn't come back. The whole household was sad. So that night, I waited until everyone was asleep to make my move. I wanted to follow the strong trail of Mikey's scent that I had picked up before. Standing all alone in the silent woods on an eerie moonlit night, I wished Rufus was here. I hadn't seen him all day. It was bitter cold and I was tired from my fight with the coyote, but I had to find Mikey.

I walked along several streets that were packed with snow. The scent took me to different houses where Mikey had stopped. He probably had to go to the bathroom. An owl, perched above, hooted and flew away. The illuminated eyes of rabbits and deer glowed at me. My spine tingled with both terror and excitement. It had taken all of my courage to brave the cold and darkness. A kaleidoscope of mysterious smells bombarded me. Just as Mikey's trail went cold, there was a faint noise from somewhere in the distance. I tried to pinpoint it, but it was so low I couldn't make it out. Even though I was fascinated wandering around in this strange new place, I was relieved that the howling wind pushing at my back, quickly blew me toward Aunt Lulu's home.

I hope I can sneak back in without being caught.

I crawled through the doggie door. Fortunately, the house was still. I was so cold. I went to the bedroom where we were staying. Mom and Dad were fast asleep. The fireplace was crackling and giving out some warmth. My last thought before I fell asleep was…

Mikey, where could you be?

Chapter Nine

I smelled cookies and pies. Was I dreaming? I went into the kitchen. Aunt Lulu gave me a slice of an apple. The aroma of apples, pumpkin and cinnamon hung in the air. She and Mom were cooking a big turkey for Thanksgiving dinner. Plates full of yummy smelling things were on the table. The phone rang several times.

Aunt Lulu sighed and wiped her eyes, "I can't believe no one has spotted Mikey yet."

Mom hugged her. "Lulu, don't give up. We'll keep looking."

After dinner, I jumped up on the sofa and climbed into Aunt Lulu's lap. I wanted her to not be so sad, so I kept licking her face.

A little later, I ran into Rufus. We were both outside doing our business, when he said, "Jaxx, let's look for Mikey tonight, okay?"

"We might as well," I said. "He's still nowhere to be seen."

I was getting to be an expert at sneaking out. This time, Rufus was waiting for me out front, as we'd planned. Climbing the crest of a hill we picked up Mikey's scent. The hazy sky made it easier for us to remain hidden. The cold air took my breath away. Rufus was panting heavily and wheezing.

"Rufus, are you all right? Do you need to stop?"

"No, I'm okay, Jaxx. Just out of shape. I figured out a shortcut to Mikey's trail. Follow me."

We walked along a snow packed path. Suddenly the shifting sounds of ice began to crack beneath me.

"Run, Rufus! Run!"

I scampered away just in time. Rufus went down on all fours and was lying sprawled out on the ice, just as the surface beneath him gave way.

"JAXX, JAXX! HELP ME!"

He fell through the thin ice and sank into the freezing cold pond. Rufus grabbed onto the edge of the ice, but fell in again and again. He was gasping for air!

"Hwooow! Hwooow! Hwooow! Hwooow! Hwooow!" My howling was really a desperate plea for help.

Rufus struggled to keep his head above water.

A car approached. I ran toward it to get help. The hairs went up on my back. *It was Dad!*

He yelled out the car window, "Jaxx! I've been driving all over looking for you. First, Mikey disappears, and now you!"

"Arf! Arf! Arf!"

I got close to the car and then darted away.

"Jaxx!" Dad hollered, "Come here!"

But I didn't listen. He parked the car, and got out. I raced to where Rufus was struggling to stay afloat. Dad chased after me and spotted Rufus.

"Oh, my gosh!" Dad cried out, "Just hold on!"

I stayed near Rufus. He was shivering. He kept going under. My heart was pounding.

I pleaded, "Rufus, keep your head above water. And try to keep moving your legs!"

Dad dragged a large tree branch to the outside of the pond. I was afraid he'd slip and fall through the ice, too. Dad crawled on his stomach and got close to the edge. He held the branch out to Rufus.

"Rufus," I yelled, "get on the branch!"

"I can't. I can't feel my legs."

"Rufus, DO IT!"

I raced around a dry patch of ground nearby like I was in a wild hornet's nest. I said silent prayers.

"Rufus, grab onto the branch! NOW!"

With one gasping lunge, Rufus pulled himself up and over the branch. Dad crawled backwards on his stomach, dragging the branch, and Rufus, away from the pond and broken ice.

Rufus' eyes rolled back into his head. Dad picked him up and then got me. He wrapped us both with his jacket. Dad opened the car door and put me into my crate. He put Rufus on his lap, tapped him on the chest and blew breaths into his nose. My heart was breaking.

"Uhm. Uhm." I began to whimper.

"Don't cry, Jaxx. I'm taking your friend to the hospital. But, one thing I'd sure like to know is what you two pups were up to?"

He drove like the wind. He stopped and parked at the animal hospital. I recognized it. It was the same place where Dad had put up Mikey's poster. He took me out of the crate and snapped on my leash.

"This way, Jaxx!" He rushed inside with Rufus in his arms yelling, "Help! Help!"

A man popped out of a room and came over. "What's the problem here?"

Dad handed Rufus over to the doctor. "This dog fell into a freezing pond. I think he has hypothermia. My dog Jaxx was exposed to the cold too, but was not in the water."

"Come on!" The doctor took Rufus to the hospital section. We followed him. Rufus was so cold from the freezing water, he was barely breathing. They covered him with heated blankets and were doing all kinds of things to him. A technician took my temperature and gave me a warm blanket. It felt wonderful. Dad stayed with me. I dozed off and woke up later in a cage near Rufus. The doctor introduced himself to some people standing close to Rufus. They must be his parents.

"We're doing everything we can." Dr. Nick said. "I'd like to keep him here. Why don't you go home and come back in the morning."

Rufus was sleeping. He had tubes going into his body and mouth.

Dr. Nick checked on me. "Hey, Jaxx," he whispered quietly. "How are you doing, buddy? Your dad went home. He and your mom will be back in a few hours. Go back to sleep."

I waited until everyone left the room. I whispered to Rufus, "I am so sorry you fell into the pond. You are my brave and special friend. I have to leave now to find Mikey. A promise is a promise. I'll see you later."

I unclasped my cage door. My trick, remember? I waited until it was quiet, and made my move. I jumped out and followed a path in the dark to the front of the hospital. I stepped on the automatic door opener mat, and when the front door opened up by itself, I snuck out. I was cold and tired, but Mikey was still missing.

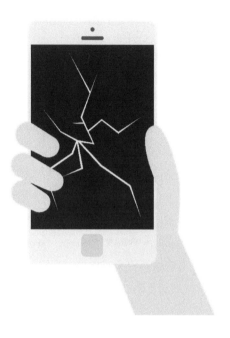

Chapter Ten

Mikey's trail led me to a big house. I knew this house. I'd been here before. It's Consuela's. My friend Colin stays here.
What are those strange smells?

I sniffed all around the house until I found an opening in a trap door in the back. I crawled inside.

It was quiet. A night light lit the hall. I climbed up the long staircase. I couldn't believe my eyes when I got to the top of the stairs.

Oh, no! Colin and his grandmother were sitting on the hallway rug, tied up.

"Jaxx!" said Colin, "What are you doing here?"

They were struggling with ropes tied around their hands and feet.

"Here boy!" He pointed his chin down. I was confused, but I did what Colin asked. I loosened the ropes with my teeth and Colin finished the job.

Consuela's ropes were tight. Colin found scissors and cut them off quickly. She was weak and unsteady.

Colin picked up a telephone. There was no dial tone.

"They must have cut the wires!" he said.

"Not only that, they smashed our cell phones," Consuela groaned, "and, they took my car keys, too! Colin, I must check on the dogs!"

Colin lifted me up, took Consuela's hand, and headed for the elevator. We got in and he pressed a button. We rode down a floor. It felt like we were riding in one of the elevators in our apartment house.

When Consuela opened the door to ZuZu, Bella, Angel and Teddy's room they barked and barked and jumped all over her and Colin.

They hugged the pups. The dogs had water and seemed okay.

"Hush, now. I'll be right back!" Consuela said.

She opened the door to Annabella's room. "OH NO!" she cried.

I ran into the room to see what was wrong. Annabella's velvet bed was empty. My heart sank.

Consuela sat down in a chair that rocked back and forth. Tears poured down her face like a rainy day. "My Annabella. What have they done with my Annabella?"

"Oh, Grammy." Colin put his arms around her and cried, too. "We'll find her."

"Colin, go get help! Take Jaxx with you. I need to stay with the other dogs. Go!"

Before we left, I jumped up on the rocker and licked Consuela's face. It was all I could think of to do.

Chapter Eleven

Colin and I made the long trek to the next door neighbor's house. He banged and banged on the door, but no answer. We trudged to the neighbor's house on the other side and banged on their door. No answer.

Colin ran up the street screaming, "Help! Help! Anybody home?"

He turned and spotted a car approaching. Colin waved his arms frantically and flagged it down.

"Please help! Help me!"

The car rolled to a stop.

Colin peered in. He signaled to the driver to roll down the window.

"OHH! Dr. Nick, am I glad to see you!"

"Dr. Nick opened the car door. "Get in, Colin. It's freezing!"

Colin picked me up and we got in.

Dr. Nick said, "I was just coming to check on Annabella. I've had a long…. Say, what are you doing out in the middle of the night, Colin? Hey, wait. Isn't that Jaxx?"

"Dr. Nick, you have to call the police!"

"What? What's happened, Colin?"

"Yesterday, some bad men tied us up. They're dangerous and have guns!"

"What?"

"It's true!"

"What's really going on, Colin?"

"I'm trying to tell you! Grammy and I were tied up by some men yesterday. We overheard them talking. Philipe, Grammy's assistant, and those men are part of a dog kidnapping gang. One of them smashed our phones and took Grammy's car keys. Then, Jaxx showed up and loosened my ropes. I was able to cut off Grammy's."

"But Colin, how was that possible? I just saw Jaxx at the hospital. I even said good night to him. How could he have been in two places at once?"

"Dr. Nick, I'm telling you the truth! I don't know how Jaxx got here, but I'm glad he did. Why would I make this up? How many times do I have to tell you? They tied us up and smashed our phones. The men are gone for now, but they could return anytime. I'm worried that Grammy's all alone in the house with the dogs. And Annabella is missing and was probably kidnapped, too. And you know, she's going to have her pups any day. One of the men said that they are going to sell Grammy's show dogs and Annabella's pups as soon as they're born. The workmen around her house are part of the dog kidnapping gang, too!" Grammy made us go for help. You have to call 911 now!"

Dr. Nick's forehead wrinkled in disbelief.

"Look, Dr. Nick, you either believe me or you don't. But either way, call the police!"

Dr. Nick picked up his phone and dialed 911.

As Dr. Nick turned into Consuela's circular driveway, the car skidded sideways on the ice. I was on Colin's lap in the front seat. Dr. Nick tried to avoid the ice while navigating the driveway toward Consuela's house. We skidded once more and ended up right in front of Consuela's garage.

Gong! Gong! Sirens, and security alarms rang out. The flashing floodlights illuminated the whole yard like the Fourth of July. They lit up the garage and our car. Strange men were carrying crates and shoving them into two cars. The shrieking cries of terrified dogs were all around us. The sound of so much barking made me scared, too. *Would I be taken next?*

"Hurry up!" one of the men shouted. "We gotta get out of here!"

The cars raced out of the garage, headed straight for us. Their blinding lights made my hair bristle. Dr. Nick started up the car, shifted it into reverse, and quickly backed out of their oncoming path. He drove in the opposite direction, toward Consuela's street entrance. One of the cars was gaining on us. Our tires spun on the ice again. Dr. Nick steered out of a slide and did his best to drive around slippery and treacherous patches. He stopped the car. I could see bright lights getting closer. A man got out of a car that was parked in front of ours. He pulled out his gun as he walked towards Dr. Nick, and aimed it at him.

"Don't move! Who sent you?"

The man's phone went off. He spoke into it. "Yeah? Yeah, we're leaving now!"

Dr. Nick pushed Colin and me to the floor. Before he could answer, the man shouted, "If you wanna stay alive, don't follow!" He tucked his gun back into his coat pocket, got in his car and drove into the street. The other car followed.

I was shaking so hard I thought I'd break into pieces. Police sirens were blaring.

Colin squeezed me tight. "It's all right, Jaxx," he said, terrified and shaking, too. "We're safe now."

Police cars raced up the street and barricaded the kidnappers' cars. Several police officers jumped out of their cars and pointed their guns at them. One of them shouted, "Drop your weapons and come out with your hands up! Put 'em up so we can see them!"

The thieves did what they were told. They were handcuffed and taken away. The police began to search through the kidnapper's cars. A couple of the policemen came running over to our car. One officer inquired, "You folks okay?"

Dr. Nick nodded 'yes'.

The other one asked, "Excuse me, sir. Are you the vet? We could use your assistance with all these animals."

"Yes, I'm Dr. Nick. I'll be right with you."

"Colin, I'm going to help the police," he said. "Hopefully, I'll find Annabella. Do you want to come with me?"

"Well, um… I wish I could, Dr. Nick. But first, I have to find Grammy and stay with her."

I wanted to go with Dr. Nick to look for Annabella, and check on the dogs, but I decided to stay with Colin. We watched as the police searched the garage, before they went into Consuela's house. When they got the all clear sign, the police escorted us inside.

"Your grandmother is safe," one of the officers said to Colin. "She wants to see you."

As we headed for the stairs, Philipe came into view at the top. He was fighting with two men. One man punched him in the face. Philipe fell to the floor, but sprang back up quickly. As he wrestled with the man, the other guy jumped on Philipe's back. Philipe swung around, and slammed his back into the wall. The man could not cling to Philipe's neck any longer and fell to the floor. Philipe grabbed them and handcuffed them both. A few policemen assisted Philipe and led the thieves away to a police car.

Philipe spoke into his walkie-talkie. "Yes sir, this is Detective Marlowe. I caught the ringleader of the dog kidnapping gang and one of his accomplices. They are all in custody."

Colin and I raced upstairs. Philipe told us to follow him. Consuela was sitting in a large room. She was talking to a policeman who was writing in his notebook. Colin ran over to her and hugged her tightly.

"Grammy!" Colin said, crying, "I was so worried about you! Dr. Nick is here. He picked up Jaxx and me on the street and called the police. And Philipe is really a detective?"

"Consuela," Detective Philipe said, "I'm sorry for the terrible fright I put you and Colin through. I couldn't tell you I was an undercover detective. This dognapping ring was stealing dogs from breeders who only have champion and purebred dogs. To throw off suspicion, they've been stealing dogs from neighboring towns; not just Barkhamsted."

"You sure fooled me, Detective Philipe! You have done a great job with my dogs. How do you know so much about them?"

"My parents were dog breeders. They bred Golden Retrievers. I have been around dogs all my life. I have my own and love them. So when I saw your ad about needing an assistant for your show dogs, I knew it would be a perfect set up for me to go undercover and find the kidnappers."

"Where were you when those horrible men tied us up?" she asked.

"I'm sorry that I wasn't here when that happened. I was out searching for the kidnapped pups. We had to find them and we did, but there are kidnapped pups still missing. They were selling the dogs to people online and all over the world, and intended to sell yours. Fortunately, we caught the thieves and they are going to be sent to prison for a long time!"

Consuela turned to Detective Philipe, "I don't know if I should be furious with you for deceiving me or hug you for saving the stolen pups! But, she cried out, "Where's my Annabella? What did they do with her?"

Detective Philipe's phone rang. "Excuse me," he said. "Yes, sir. A-huh. A-huh. Yes, have him come up."

Dr. Nick came in carrying Annabella. He carefully placed her at Consuela's feet, on the carpeted floor.

Consuela sobbed, "My Annabella! Annabella! Oh, thank goodness!"

She and Colin kept hugging her. I licked her, myself, several times. Annabella was very quiet.

Detective Philipe said, "I was just informed that the rest of the kidnapped dogs are in the old fruit cellar out back!"

Colin said, "I know where it is! I'll show you the way. Grammy, I'll be back as soon as I can."

I said to Annabella, "I'm going to help find the pups. But, I'll see you later." I nuzzled her nose.

"Oh good, Jaxx."

Detective Philipe, several officers, and Dr. Nick followed us. Strange sounds and scents drifted towards me as we all made our way out the back door and across the snow-covered yard. We went through a doorway down into a tunnel. It was dark and scary. Inside the damp and dark chamber were fifteen metal crates lined up against a wall, each one contained a puppy. They were all whimpering, howling and barking non-stop.

Those are the sounds I heard before

The men stood there in silence. The pups terror and fear filled the air. Some pups were standing on their hind legs, biting furiously on the metal cage doors, desperate to get out.

"I want to go home?" one puppy cried. "Where's my mommy?"

I felt sick to my stomach that they had been wrenched away from their families.

"Please, don't cry. Everything is okay, now." I said to the frightened puppies.

Dr. Nick and Colin grabbed some bottles of water that were in cartons and filled the water bowls in their cages. The thirsty puppies drank greedily. Colin reached his fingers in to stroke their tiny heads.

"MEOW! MEOW!"

My ears perked up. Those meows sounded familiar. I looked around, then followed my nose. Way in the back, I peeked behind some crates and sniffed some more. A cat suddenly jumped down out of the shadows and licked my nose! I couldn't believe it. MIKEY WAS HERE!

"Hey Jaxx! What took you so long?" said Mikey.

"Mikey, you gave us quite a scare. We've all been looking for you. Aunt Lulu hasn't stopped crying since you went missing!"

"Serves me right, Jaxx, for nosing around and getting locked up down here."

"Good news. You're going home, Mikey!"

Chapter Twelve

Detective Philipe, Dr. Nick and several policemen finished loading the fifteen rescued pups and their crates, into a police van. In addition, there were six stolen pups they had rescued from the thieves' getaway cars. Fortunately, Annabella had been one of them. There was going to be a police escort to the animal hospital.

Dr. Nick remained behind. He had received a message from Consuela to meet her in Annabella's room right away. Colin and I followed him. Consuela was seated near Annabella. Annabella was panting hard and pacing back and forth. She rested in between. Dr. Nick examined her and said quietly, "You're about to give birth any moment, young lady! Consuela, and Colin, you'll both be assisting me. Colin, please take Jaxx out into the hallway, now."

It was my turn to pace back and forth.

After a while, Dr. Nick, Consuela and Colin came out. They were all smiling.

Dr. Nick phoned Detective Philipe and announced, "Annabella just had five puppies. Mother and pups are all doing well. I'll meet you at the animal hospital as soon as I'm done here." After he hung up, Dr. Nick told Colin how important it was that Annabella gets her rest. "She's been through a lot. So, no visitors for the time being. It's just you and your grandmother. Stay here and help her while I go to the hospital to check on the rescued puppies, okay?"

"Sure! Okay, Dr. Nick."

I inched toward the doorway to Anabella's room. But before I could sneak in, Dr. Nick lifted me up into his arms. "Jaxx, I need to examine you, too. You've had quite an adventure!"

Back at the hospital, we were greeted by Mom, Dad and Aunt Lulu. Mom and Dad kept hugging me a lot.

"MIKEY!" Aunt Lulu cried out, tearfully embracing her beloved missing cat, after Dr. Nick placed him in her arms.

The police brought the kidnapped pups to the examining room. While the technicians and Dr. Nick examined the pups, the police photographer documented each one. Since the pups didn't have microchips, they were cross referenced with the breeders who came forward. Detective Philipe reassured everyone that all of the kidnapped dogs would be reunited with their owners.

After I was examined and declared healthy, Dr. Nick brought me over to see Rufus. His tail was wagging.

"Hiya, Jaxx!"

"Hi, Rufus! I'm so happy you are feeling better. I'm sure you heard we found Mikey. And the missing puppies are safe."

"What missing puppies?" Rufus, asked.

"Oh, Wow! You missed the part about the guys who kidnapped lots of purebred dogs from breeders around here. I'll tell you all about it later. Let's just say my promise to you to help find Mikey, led me to the right place. So you were a part of rescuing Mikey and the kidnapped pups, as well!"

Chapter Thirteen

I was walking down the hall at the animal hospital with my parents, after my visit with Rufus. I passed by a cage that had a puppy inside that looked just like me. I walked back and took another look to make sure I wasn't imagining it. A little dog was hiding in the back trembling. It was very strange looking at my mirror image, but a younger me. He had feathery white hair, a black button nose, and a white splash of a mustache. He was thin and had a bandaged paw.

"Hello. Who are you?" I asked.

"I'm Beau."

"Hi Beau. I'm Jaxx. Why are you here?"

In between sobs, Beau gasped, "I got separated from my family when there was a terrible flood. I was rescued. They brought me to this place. People walk back and forth past my cage, but I don't recognize anyone. It's hard to sleep without my family and favorite pillow. The people are nice, but I'm scared about what might happen next? I don't like being alone."

I snuggled as close as I could to his cage and stayed until he fell asleep. There was something special about him and I didn't want to leave, but I had to. It was time to go back to Aunt Lulu's.

I hope I'll see him again.

Chapter Fourteen

Something was going on. Mom and Aunt Lulu were busy in the kitchen and Dad was building the crackling fire in the living room fireplace. They talked about people coming over to the house to celebrate the holiday. Mikey was home safe and sound. There was a knock at the front door.

Dad said, "I'll get it!"

"Arf! Arf! Arf!"

"Quiet, Jaxx. Let's see who's here."

Dad opened the door.

"Colin! Dr. Nick! Please come in and join the party!"

Dad took everyone's coats. Dr. Nick handed Dad a large container that was covered. Dad left the room with it, and came back empty handed.

Colin rushed over and gave me a big hug. "Hi Jaxx! How are you doing, boy?"

I did my happy dance around him. I was still dancing when I saw Rufus and his parents.

"Rufus, I'm so glad to see you! How are you?"

"I'm doing great, Jaxx, now that we won't be sneaking out at night anymore!"

He laughed in his own wheezing bulldog way.

Colin said to Dad, "Grammy stayed back to take care of Annabella and her puppies."

"How's Annabella doing?" Dad asked.

"She's nursing her babies. Soon she'll be able to have visitors. Grammy said Jaxx can visit Annabella in a few days."

Did I hear my name and Annabella's? Oh Boy!

Mom came into the living room carrying a tray of goodies, and said, "Hello everyone. I hope you can all stay for a while."

Dr. Nick saw Colin on the floor with me and said, "Colin, you have a special way with animals. A real gift. I believe you have a future as a veterinarian. When you're a little older, I'd like you to volunteer at our hospital, whenever you're in town."

"Wow!" said Colin. "I'd like that a lot. Gee, thanks, Dr. Nick."

Just then, Aunt Lulu clapped her hands. "Everyone, Dr. Nick would like to say something."

Dr. Nick reached for the large container that Dad handed over to him.

"Jaxx! Come here, boy! I have something for you." He removed a blanket cover and there in a crate was Beau wagging his feathery tail. I was over the moon! Beau climbed out of his crate and ran up to me. I couldn't get over the resemblance. He looked just like me, but smaller. Mom and Dad hugged him and I licked his face. He kept licking me back.

"Arf! Arf! Arf!"

I was so happy I ran circles around Dr. Nick, Mom and Dad, and Aunt Lulu. I had a little brother!

Chapter Fifteen

A week later, on the train ride home, Beau's crate was in Dad's lap. Mine was in Mom's. As I looked out the window and saw peoples' houses, I didn't have to wonder who lived in them anymore. We'll be coming back to Barkhamsted in a few weeks to celebrate the holidays with Aunt Lulu and Mikey. I'll get to see Rufus and Tom Tom. I am looking forward to seeing Annabella and her pups at Consuela's. Colin will be there, too.

I thought about all the new adventures Beau and I were going to have.

If you open up your heart, and take chances, life can lead you on different and exciting journeys.

Acknowledgments

Special thanks to the people of Barkhamsted, a beautiful town in Litchfield County, Connecticut, USA, that is the centerpiece of my book. Please excuse the poetic license I took at times, to change some things to fit the story.

My deepest gratitude to:

Linda Chiara, my extraordinary editor and "Northern Star," whose expert guidance always keeps me on the right path.

Ashley Fontainne, One of a Kind Covers, for her brilliant and stunning designs and creative vision.

Marcia Madeira, my 24/7 all-knowing technical advisor and loyal friend.

Arlene Buckley, for her unceasing belief, keen insights and dedication.

My beloved husband Jeffrey, my rock, for his constant encouragement and love.

A special thanks to the following people for their unwavering support and friendship:

Sarah and Cole Ahearn; Lucy and Peter Ascoli; Joseph Battisti; Don and Jane Bermont; Wendy, Peter, and Parker Bernstein; Rosemarie and Rick Brower; Arlene, June, and Tom Buckley; Chris and Lou Cook; Marsha Casper Cook; Demaree Cooney; Susan Diamond; Sara and Charles Dossick; Ron, Rose, Peggy, and Christina Doster; Tammie, Jackie and Justine Duong; Aton Edwards; Martin, Terry,

Dayna, Leah and Marley Egan; Elizabeth, Brett, and Adam Erickson; Dr. Mark Estren; Chris, Chloe and Elyse Harbert; Donelda and John Hawley; Dr. Frank Hermantin; Dr. David Kellman; James Klein; Lloyd Korn; Mia, Maxi, and Stanford Kravitz; Chuck Kreske III; Cyndy and Lee Landgraver; Gerardo Lara; Skyler Egan Miller; Phillip and Ruth Miller; Nancy Mizels; John Monteleone; Kathryn Moran; Roberta Parry; Sam and Gladys Piazza; Erin, Steve, and William Reardon; Nancy Rebehn; Megan, Ryan, and Florence Richardson; Kathy Rosenblatt; Dr. Jennifer Rubin; Linda Stein; Bernice Stone; Yonatan Tsapira; Chanel and William Tucker; Helen Weber; Krissy Weiser; Elizabeth, Alicia, and James Wong; and Nancy Wright.

My heartfelt thanks to:

Litchfield Veterinary Hospital CT; Veterinary Emergency of Canton CT; Muddy Moose Mutts Rescue of Winsted CT; Winchester/Winsted Animal Control CT; Torrington Animal Control CT; New Hartford/Barkhamsted Animal Control CT; Hartford Animal Shelter CT; Angell Memorial Animal Hospital, MA; Buddy Dog Humane Society, Inc. MA; and to all of the other saviors and rescuers of animals all over the world.

Credits

I wish to thank the following illustrators and providers whose contributions helped make this story come to life:

Cover: Shutterstock/ Razvan Ionut Dragomirescu; Puskin.

Can Stock Photo Inc.: AlexanderPokusay.

Istockphoto.com: Pobytov.

Pixaby.com

Pngtree.com

Shutterstock.com: rvika; pio3; AlenaPo; Kuznetsov Alexey; robuart; Ramanava Yauheniya; Evgenii Skorniakov; Yuliya Art; Nadia Snopek; theflashlife; Sabelskaya; Bukavik.

About the Author

Joanna Lee Doster, published author of *Tails Of Jaxx At The Metropolitan Opera*, (MPI); *Maximum Speed: Pushing The Limit*, (MPI); and *Celebrity Bedroom Retreats*, (Rockport); is also a freelance journalist.

She has worked for television production companies and held executive positions in cable television programming networks such as: Arts & Entertainment, The Learning Channel, and PBS.

She lives in Connecticut.

CPSIA information can be obtained
at www.ICGtesting.com
Printed in the USA
LVHW072134131219
639778LV00015B/128/P

* 9 7 8 0 9 9 6 0 1 7 9 6 1 *